Published by Ladybird Books Ltd
27 Wrights Lane London W8 5TZ
A Penguin Company
3 5 7 9 10 8 6 4 2
© Ladybird Books Ltd MCMXCIX

Printed in Italy

Disney's

Winnie the Pooh

and Tigger too

Tigger loved to bounce. "Bouncing is what Tiggers do best!" he told all his friends. One day, when Rabbit was working in his vegetable garden, Tigger came bouncing by. He bounced so hard that he knocked Rabbit over.

"I'm tired of your bouncing," said Rabbit. "Why can't you stop?"

The next day, Rabbit, Pooh, Piglet and Tigger decided to explore the forest. Tigger bounced ahead as usual.

"It's time to un-bounce Tigger once and for all," Rabbit told Pooh and Piglet. "I have a plan. Follow me."

Rabbit led Pooh and Piglet into a hollow tree trunk. "We're going to lose Tigger," he explained.

"But why?" asked Pooh.

"So that he will be grateful when we find him again," said Rabbit. "Then he will be a humble, unbouncy Tigger!"

Tigger came back to look for his friends. "Halloo!" he called. But they didn't answer him, and at last he bounced away.

When they were sure Tigger was gone, the three friends started to walk home.

"We'll come back for Tigger tomorrow – and he will be unbounced for ever!" said Rabbit.

It was a long way back, and Pooh and Piglet were tired. While they stopped to rest, Rabbit went on by himself.

But as Rabbit walked through the misty forest, he realised that he was lost! It was getting dark, and there were strange noises all around.

"Shish-rustle-crunch."

"Who's that?" cried Rabbit. But it was only a caterpillar chewing a leaf.

"Grr-AWK!" gulped a frog.

"Help!" cried Rabbit.

All at once Rabbit heard a familiar bounce-bounce-bouncing sound. It was Tigger!

"Halloo, Rabbit!" said Tigger. "Shall I take you home? It's very late to be out in the forest!"

So a very quiet, humble Rabbit held on to Tigger's tail as Tigger bounced all the way home.

"This really is the best way to travel, isn't it?" said Tigger.

And Rabbit had to agree.

Winter soon came and a thick blanket of snow covered The Hundred Acre Wood.

One frosty morning, Tigger bounced through the snow to Roo's house.

"Hallooo, Roo!" called Tigger. "Would you like to come and play?"

"May I, Mama?" Roo asked Kanga.

"All right," said Kanga. "But be back in time for tea!"

With Roo sitting on his shoulders,
Tigger bounced off into the snowy
forest.

"Can Tiggers climb trees?" Roo asked
his friend.

"Of course!" said Tigger. "We just
bounce up them!"

"That sounds like fun!" said Roo.
"Let's bounce up a tree together!"

So they found a tall tree, and Tigger bounced. Up… up… and up he went, up to the very top of the tree.

"I never knew trees were so high," gulped Tigger, trying not to look down.

"Wheee! This is fun!" said Roo, swinging from Tigger's tail.

"P… P… Please stop swinging," said Tigger.

"All right," said Roo, climbing onto a branch. "Shall we go home now?"

But Tigger couldn't get down. He was stuck!

Luckily, Pooh and Piglet were out walking nearby. When they saw Tigger and Roo up in the tree, they called all their friends to come and help.

"Please get me down!" groaned Tigger. "If I can just get back on the ground, I'll never bounce again!"

Christopher Robin took off his coat to make a net. "Jump, and we'll catch you!" he called. "You first, Roo."

"Wheee! Here I come!" cried Roo happily.

It was Tigger's turn next. Soon he was safe on the ground again. "I'm so happy I could bounce all the way home!" he said.

"Remember your promise," said Rabbit. "No more bouncing!"

"Oh… yes," said Tigger sadly.

"Isn't it wonderful?" exclaimed Rabbit. "No more bouncing!"

"But Tigger isn't Tigger without his bounce," said Pooh.

"Pooh's right," said Kanga. "I'd rather have the old, bouncy Tigger back."

Rabbit realised that his friends were right.

"Oh, all right," he said at last. "Come back and bounce, Tigger!"

Everyone cheered, and soon they were all bouncing together, having a wonderful time in the snow-covered Hundred Acre Wood.